FASCINATION

DANIEL BLYTHE

Fascination ISBN 978-1-78464-613-4

Text © Daniel Blythe 2016
Complete work © Badger Publishing Limited 2016

Publisher: Susan Ross
Senior Editor: Danny Pearson
Editorial Coordinator: Claire Morgan
Copyeditor: Cambridge Publishing Management
Designer: Bigtop Design Ltd
Cover: © moodboard / Alamy Stock Photo

2 4 6 8 10 9 7 5 3 1

CHAPTER 1

MAYA AND ALFIE

On the screen, I see her sweep down that golden staircase, her shiny dress jet-black and her shoes crimson. Head held high, dark hair streaming in the artificial wind.

Her eyes look wrong. Over-painted and ancient.

They've made her look like some kind of goddess. They must have given her contacts, because she'd be almost blind without her glasses.

Music thunders, an electronic fanfare. I know what it is — it's based on an old song from the 1970s, one my nan likes, called 'Hold On Tight to Your Dreams'. (We've always laughed at the bit where it goes into French for no reason. My nan says it's really bad French.)

She spreads her arms out wide, drinking in the applause. Her mouth is a big stripe of red with impossibly ice-white teeth. Her face is caked in make-up, but you'd only know it if you knew, like me, what she really looked like. A pretty girl — yeah, for those who like girls — but not one of those shiny TV goddesses, not one of those music princesses. Not Maya.

Except she is.

She is now.

They've taken her, taken Maya Barnes, my best friend since we were five, and they've turned her into something else. Something new. Something *wrong*.

They've made her into a monster.

***

My last happy memory. Me and Maya, in
the park:

"Are you doing anything this summer?" Maya
asks me.

We are sitting on the swings, like we used to as
little kids. Swinging side by side. Never quite in
harmony, meeting in the middle, laughing.

The mums with toddlers are giving us filthy looks,
wondering what these sixteen-year-olds are doing
in a kids' park, why they haven't got anywhere
else to go. They're making comments, I can tell,
about my green hair and my pierced lip.

Beyond us, there's the usual expanse of green
and grey, littered with chip-papers and Coke-
cans, and further beyond, the line of the dark
grey flats where we live. Greenwell Heights,
armpit of England.

On the other side of the hill, the city, with dark
grey clouds squatting over it as if they can't bear

to allow it to look beautiful. It can, sometimes. At sunset. With Maya, in summer, when we've had a good time, felt buzzing. Those few happy moments. Maya makes it good. Then we go and hang out at hers.

Maya's flat's always been open to me, and my family's always welcomed her. I think they thought we were 'going out'. Yeah, right. Like they haven't worked *me* out by now. Er, hello? Is the massive Tom Hiddleston poster on my wall not enough of a clue?

"Just hanging around, I guess," I reply. "Waiting to find out how many GCSEs I've failed. And trying not to get beaten up."

Maya laughs, her long dark hair streaming in the wind. "Always the optimist, Alfie."

"What about you? You stopped doing the YouTube stuff?" I bring my swing to a halt, doing my usual thing of adjusting my woollen hat, pulling it down almost over my eyes like I don't want anyone to recognise me.

In a second or two, I've got Maya's YouTube channel up on my phone.

"Oh, God," she says, twirling on the swing in embarrassment, twisting the chains. "Sometimes I think you're the only one who ever looks at that."

She doesn't think that, of course. Thousands look at it.

There she is on the screen. Maya talking, wittering on about this and that. It's what she does. Sometimes she reviews albums and downloads, sometimes she talks about books and gigs and new bands. Sometimes she plays and sings her own stuff on the guitar.

"I like this one," I tell her.

It's just Maya singing, in semi-darkness, not looking at the camera, hair falling over her glasses. She's playing the guitar, just a few simple chords.

You never forget it when you first feel like this,

It steals inside your mind and says, hey, just be damned and do it,

You never forget you 'cos you killed me with your kiss,

Chill me with your ardour like this,

Kill me, kill me, kill me with your kiss.

"Alfie, don't!" she says, laughing, trying to grab the phone off me. "Really, don't! It's… it's like embarrassing when it's just you and me."

"It's not! Don't be silly. It's really *good*."

And I start to swing again, kicking my legs high, my phone blasting Maya's song out to the playground.

***

That's the last summer day I can remember that was normal. The last happy memory, before all of it. Before the big black car, and Magnus Gold, and Zoe, and all the rest.

When I say Maya had always looked after me, I really mean it. We'd been friends for years, ever since Reception. I think she saw something in me that was like her. Not taking the easy way out. Not conforming. Wanting to play a different game. Maya and Alfie, Alfie and Maya.

That's the way it always was.

Until it all changed.

Until that day they took her away from me.

CHAPTER 2

SILVER AND GOLD

It all changed when Maya met Magnus Gold. Mr Multi-media. A man with a huge empire of music, technology, films, books, sweets, T-shirts, perfumes, shoes.

People like Magnus Gold are the new gods. Nobody goes to church any more, but they do worship at the altar of people like Magnus Gold.

He's tall, tanned and smoothly muscular, bulging out of a white silk shirt and a velvet suit. Yeah, I bet he works out. Keeps his private life pretty much under wraps, but I reckon all the women he's been out with have been paid to have short-term 'relationships' with him. He's been seen with arm-candy like Jenna Spaull and Kat Kaine. Starlets just over half his age.

I don't reckon he's interested in them.

Really. You can see it in his eyes.

He thinks of women the way I do — beautiful, sleek, dazzling company, but not for *that*. I know it. I can see these things.

It was Zoe who approached Maya first. Zoe Silver. Magnus Gold's henchwoman, his head judge, his star-picker from his Saturday night sensation *The Bomb*.

She put comments on Maya's YouTube first of all, saying how talented she thought Maya was. Of course, Maya had no idea at first who "ZoZo81" was — thought she was just another fan. Then "ZoZo81" followed her on social media, and that led to emails, and meetings.

Zoe Silver — not her real name, of course. I think her real name is something like Smith or

13

Jones. But it sounds good, doesn't it? Silver and Gold, the star-making partnership.

Zoe Silver is like a snake. She's snake-hipped and fork-tongued. She has slick silvery hair and wears reflective shades and tight glittery dresses. Wherever she goes, she looks dressed up for a night on the town. She carries a silver iPad with her everywhere, and people say it has enough information in it to bring down the BBC, the church and even the government.

She's explaining it all to Maya that time in Caffeine, the coolest coffee-bar in town, where they started having meetings. Yes, our town does have some cool places, even if most of it is concrete, curry-houses and car-parks.

They always have the same table, and it kind of becomes their unofficial office. No press or media ever bother them, not at this stage — nobody cares about our little town.

And me? I just happen to be hanging round, like I always do.

"But what do you mean?" Maya's saying, leaning back in her chair and frowning.

Zoe Silver smiles smugly. You can't see her eyes behind the silvery shades, so you can never trust the bitch.

From what I remember, this is, like, their third or fourth meeting.

The first, yeah, that was the strangest.

***

Maya's family were astonished when the limo first pulled up. Nobody drives flash cars round here except the dealers.

When Magnus Gold and Zoe Silver got out and knocked at the door, it was like a visitation from God, her mum said. Well, not for me. If I'd been there, I'd have thought, *Watch the car, Magnus Gold, it'll end up on bricks with the radio and lights stripped out.*

Maya's mum, Jen, thought they'd won a competition — tickets to see *The Bomb* being recorded or to go and see Blue Minx on tour, or something. Like, how could that have happened? Even I know you can't win a competition you've never entered.

***

"What we're thinking," Zoe says now, in the coffee shop, "is that the concept is you. You are the concept. The project is Maya."

"You mean," Maya says slowly, "that Mr Gold likes my songs? That he wants me to record some of them professionally?"

Zoe sips her orange juice and gives a little laugh.

"Your songs," she says, as if trying to keep a straight face. "Yes. On YouTube. Hmmm."

"Yes," replies Maya, her big eyes shining, looking from Zoe to me and back again. I shrug helplessly.

"This isn't about your songs, Maya. It's about… well, the essential *spirit* of you, really. It's about being who you are, and selling that to people. Once you're the brand, we don't need anything else. You don't need to produce a product."

"It all sounds well dodge to me," I say. Unlike Maya, I've never had a problem with speaking my mind to Zoe Silver, or anyone else.

"Thankfully, Alfie," says Zoe Silver haughtily, "this isn't about what you think, or what you want. It's about Maya." She puts on a sickly-sweet silvery smile. "Isn't it, Maya?" Zoe glances over my shoulder. "And look, here's the man himself."

Magnus Gold has slipped in without being noticed, and he's walking towards us now, all teeth and tan. He is wearing his usual showbiz shades, but apart from that, it seems it's dress-down Friday. He's wearing jeans and a West Ham shirt. I look him up and down, and cannot help sneering at him a little.

"Mineral water," he barks, without even looking at the waitress. "Chilled. Still, not sparkling. No lemon, no ice. If you put lemon or ice in it, I *will* close you down."

That's Magnus Gold all over. All charm.

He slides smoothly into the chair next to Maya and puts a brown A4 envelope on to the table. "I think we can start to talk contracts," he says in his honeyed voice. His golden voice. "I know you probably don't have a lawyer. Don't worry — I can buy you one."

His mineral water arrives and he doesn't even say thank you. I try to exchange a sympathetic look with the waitress. She doesn't respond. She doesn't seem to have recognised him.

I nod at Magnus Gold's West Ham shirt. "Didn't have you pegged as a Hammers fan, Mr Gold."

"What?" He looks vaguely irritated. "Oh, that." He waves a hand, laughing with a flash of white teeth.

"Payet's done well this season," I offer, lifting my glass to clink it with his.

Magnus Gold sighs. "Sorry, look — who *are* you?"

"This is Alfie," says Zoe Silver smoothly. "Alfie's Maya's best friend. He wants to make sure everything's all above board, don't you, Alfie?"

I feel the wind taken out of my sails a bit. I was going to show up Magnus Gold for never having even heard of West Ham's top-scoring midfielder, Dimitri Payet, but now the moment's gone.

I realise, now, how clever Zoe Silver can be, and why Magnus Gold — who is a shrewd businessman, perhaps, but not really all that clever — keeps her around.

They're a team. A very powerful team.

"Here's to the future," says Magnus Gold, and smiles. Gleaming white, like an animal baring its fangs.

Maya, for a second, looks terrified. And then she smiles too.

CHAPTER 3

THE MONSTER

A huge billboard looms out of the mist as I trudge through the estate on my early morning paper round.

I barely look up from shoving the papers into the letterboxes. It's cold. My breath mists in the air and my face and fingers go numb. It's a real grind and I hate getting up at six in the morning for it — but it means I get a bit of money.

I'm at college now, having scraped a few GCSEs over the summer. Just enough to do the Art and Design BTEC I wanted to do. Then, perhaps, I might just get on a course that gets me out of this town.

The extra cash is useful. People laugh at me for still having a paper round at nearly seventeen when I could have a proper job, but it works for me. I'm not good with people. And with my hair and attitude, who's gonna employ me in a café or a shop? There's nothing much going round here, anyway. The few part-time jobs there are get snapped up.

Nobody's going to wander into my life and offer to transform it.

I thrust the *Daily Mail* into no. 37's letterbox with a growl and as I turn round, the giant Maya looks up at me from the side of the house. And winks.

The billboard's been here since I was a little kid, looming over the back-to-back houses. It's had ads on it for TV shows, chocolate, shampoo. But this is the first time it's been digital. And the first time it's had Maya on it.

It's just her face, doing a digital wink — her pixels of hair blowing in the computerised wind.

And it just says MAYA.

That's all it needs to say.

Everyone knows who she is now.

***

Two months after she was swept away to London, for whatever goes on in Magnus Gold's office and in his studios, I'm in the living-room of my auntie's flat, playing around with my phone.

I haven't heard from her.

They keep her at a distance. Zoe Silver's secretary fields my calls. And they've blocked me on Twitter.

My auntie's is often a place to escape to, but today I made the wrong decision. Little cousins are running around, making the usual racket. Kyle's bashing a biscuit tin over and over, the TV's blaring, and Jayde's running round without even a nappy on so I'm afraid for the carpet.

Auntie Trish is talking loudly on the phone in the kitchen — almost shouting — to whoever her current bloke is.

Kyle points at the TV. "Look, Alfie! Maya!"

"What?" I look up, startled. And yes, it is her — being interviewed on the couch by Fearne Cotton. All glossy smiles and teeth. I scrabble around for the remote, turn up the volume.

"Maya on the telly!" screams Kyle, and starts bashing his drum even more loudly.

"Kyle!" I snap. "Keep it down!"

"— amazing rise to fame," Fearne is saying. "You've really just come from nowhere, haven't you?"

Maya giggles. She *simpers*. God, I hate that. She never used to do that.

"I suppose so," she says. "You know, I am who I am. People have to take me as they find me."

She doesn't even sound like her any more. Her voice sounds polished, robotic.

I stare at her, look into her eyes. Her eyes no longer laugh. They no longer sparkle. It's like I don't know who she is any more.

"Do you sometimes feel, Maya," Fearne is saying now, "that it's not really happening? Like it's all happening to someone else?"

Maya nods quickly. "Yes," she says. "Yes, I do. I feel like that a lot."

Like it's all happening to someone else.

Yes. That says it all.

As the weeks have gone on, the extent of what Gold has done really strikes me. I have to admit, it's quite clever.

***

He's realised that all these people who get instant fame, like the Kardashians and YouTubers and

so on, it *doesn't matter* what they actually do,
or who they are. The promotion, the brand,
the personality, they all work together, they all
become one. They're the same thing.

All that matters is that they are known, and then
they can have anything. They can have everything.

I can't have everything. I have to do a stupid
paper round and a stupid BTEC if I want to
escape from this godforsaken town.

I hate myself. I am starting to feel jealous
of Maya.

***

One night, in my bedroom, I find that her old
YouTube channel has gone. All her quirky
reviews, her silly stories and her beautiful songs.
Vanished. Gold must have had them taken down.

It's like Maya's past is disappearing. Melting. Like
icebergs losing chunks into the sea.

"You're obsessed with that Maya," says Liam crossly, sitting on my bed and scowling. He's a cute IT-geek boy from college. Floppy hair and glasses. We're not going out, but we could be. I'm allowing him to think I find him interesting for a bit. "Are you sure you're not straight, Alfie?"

"Got a problem with us being friends?" I ask, not looking up from my phone.

"Not with you being *friends*," Liam says. "Just with you always having to bring everything back to her. Maya this, Maya that. If I said I liked cheese you'd say, 'Ooh, I wonder what Maya's favourite cheese is', and you'd go and look it up."

I feel myself blushing, anger prickling through me. "That's so not true," I snap.

"Whatever," says Liam, with an icy edge to his voice. "Let me know when you're over her, Alfie." He grabs his jacket off the bed and starts to leave.

"Liam, I'm sorry," I start, putting my phone down. But he's already thumping down the stairs. I hear the door slam.

A few seconds later, my sister puts her frizzy head round the door. Kate is twenty-four, with a job at the Housing Office, but she can't afford to move out yet. She must have just got back from work. She's wearing that horrible polyester blouse with her name-badge on. She smells of cheap perfume.

"Trouble with lover-boy?" she says with a smile.

"No." I scowl, don't look at her.

"She's not coming back, you know."

I look up sharply. "Who?"

"You know who I mean," she says. "It's like Darius Kendall in my year from school." Kate grins. "Remember?"

"Not really."

"Got signed up for City when he was seventeen, left all his old mates behind. Moved to Essex. Started hanging out in Sugar Hut and dating busty blondes. And where is he now?"

Darius Kendall? I can barely remember him ever even scoring a goal for City. "No idea. Where is he now?"

"Exactly," says Kate, and nods as if that proves everything. "There's no magic wand, you know. Yeah, Magnus Gold sticks his big nose into our estate and plucks Maya out, like she's gotta be rescued or something. Well, sorry, mate, but I'm from Greenwell Heights too, and I don't need rescuing."

I realise what she is thinking. "I'm not jealous of Maya, you know."

"Really? You act like it. You're obsessed with her. And with her life, and the fact that it doesn't involve you anymore. And you're stuck here, in Boringville."

"Kate—"

My sister taps her name-badge. "This, yeah, might be boring, right? I might have to drink horrible tea, and get up when it's dark. I get the stinking bus into town and get called a bitch and a cow by the people I'm trying to help."

"I know, Kate. I really do."

"But I'm not taking anything for granted, yeah? This is life. I'm not expecting some Fairy Godfather to swan in and take me off to Showbiz Hogwarts. I'm doing it *myself*."

Easy for her to say, of course. She's bright. She did well at school. She kept her head down and didn't do all the partying the other girls did. She got A Levels, got a diploma, got a job. And that was a few years ago when it was all a bit easier.

"Look," Kate says, sitting on my bed. "You say Gold's made Maya into a monster."

"How do you know that?" I snap.

She sighs. "I do read Twitter, Alfie. All your rants."

"Oh." I look a little shamefaced. "That."

"Yeah, *that*. But you know what? I reckon he's made you a monster too, Alfie. You just don't realise it yet. Think about that."

She turns and stalks off.

I glower at her retreating back, her horrible blouse and her frizzy hair. *Get some straighteners*, I think, snarkily.

CHAPTER 4

CONNECTIONS

It's crazy. The whole country's gone Maya-mad. It's like they've forgotten she's just this ordinary girl from Greenwell Heights — or they never even knew it in the first place.

It's like they *own* this new version of her, because they own her *stuff*. Maya laminate badges on ribbons are the in-thing among the girls at college. I see them swinging from bags and necks as they pass me. With the younger kids I see around the estate, it's fluffy Maya pencil-cases and strawberry bath-bombs. There is even — God help us — an album.

I stand there in the corridor, leaning against the lockers, listening to it on Spotify on my headphones. Every so often I sneakily glance up, to make sure nobody is catching me doing this.

It is completely awful. It's obviously been put together by Gold's monkeys. There are dreadful dance covers of the Vaccines' 'If You Wanna' and Carly Rae Jepsen's 'I Really Like You'. There's string-heavy versions of ballads, older stuff, like Oasis and Mariah Carey songs. Her own simple, gentle, beautiful songs are nowhere to be seen. She doesn't even look like herself in videos and photos.

How has this happened? And how has it all happened so *quickly*? It's like Magnus Gold is in league with the dark arts. Like he's got her to sell her soul.

A message pings in. I click on it half-heartedly. It's from Liam. He's over at the college's other site today.

just for u. i kno how much she means 2 u.
sorry bout the other day. L x

There's a link. I click on it, and gasp loudly
in amazement.

It's a cached version of Maya's original YouTube
channel. I scroll down. All her posts are there —
the quirky, cute stuff, the book reviews, the songs.
How did he get this? I'm sure Gold had it all
taken off the Net. I text him back.

OMG! how u get hold of this?!

I'm shaking as I look up and down the bustling
corridor, waiting for his reply. Some people from
my course wave and nod to me as they go past.
I barely see them. Liam's message pings in.

just call it skill. dark web. ;-) c ya later

Dark Web? Yeah, right. Isn't that all drug deals
and arms and stuff? Still, I'm grateful. And I
don't want Liam to think I am not.

I click on the video with my favourite song
of hers.

With *the* song.

You never forget it when you first feel like this,

*It steals inside your mind and says, hey, just be damned
and do it,*

You never forget you, 'cos you killed me with your kiss,

Chill me with your ardour like this,

Kill me, kill me, kill me with your kiss.

You always remember when you first feel the chill,

It shivers inside you and say, hey, just be you and do it,

You never forget because I killed you with my kiss,

Thrill me with the meaning of this,

Kill me, kill me, kill me with your kiss…

A shock at home-time. Maya messages me. She wants to FaceTime.

I sit on the roundabout in the playground, ignoring the glaring mums again. Spinning round, holding my phone high so Maya gets to see a changing background.

It's so good to see her, hear her. She looks like her normal self. Hair tied back in a scrunchie, eyes soft and kind, none of that harsh TV make-up.

"Are you happy?" I ask her. "I want you to be happy."

"Of course I am, Alfie." She smiles, but not with her eyes.

"I suppose he's paying you well."

She laughs. "Mr Gold's people take care of all that. I don't even carry cash any more. How stupid is that?"

"Yeah. Stupid."

I try to think of any news that she will want to hear. Anything that will mean something in her new world, that won't sound pathetic and banal. Little Kyle's started Reception. Maddie Mills got caught snogging Mr Bentley's brother. My mum's drinking again.

Nope. None of it.

"Look," she says, and glances to one side, off-stage, as if checking she is not being listened to. "Do you want to meet up? Just… chat, you know?"

My heart surges in delight. But it is brought down by the dark, heavy realisation that she's just being nice. She doesn't want her old life back. She doesn't want me back.

She is Brand Maya now. She is a multi-media goddess. There is nothing I can give her which Mr Gold can't buy her a hundred times over. Nothing at all.

"Really?" I ask. I try not to sound too surprised.

"Really, Alfie. I can do incognito. There's a driver who will help."

"A driver. OK."

"I may have to wear a wig. Sorry."

I burst out laughing at the idea. Like Maya is in some kind of spy thriller and I am meeting her to hand over secret papers. "A wig?"

"Yeah, I know. Some kind of disguise, anyway. Unless you want to be interrupted every two minutes by squealing eleven year-olds wanting me to sign their pencil-cases?"

I can see her point.

We arrange when and where to meet. For the next twenty-four hours, I can barely contain myself.

CHAPTER 5

CRASH AND BURN

She actually does wear a wig. An electric blue wig and mirrored sunglasses just like Magnus Gold's.

We sit on either side of the table in the vegetarian café, Cakes and Kale, where we used to hang out. Nobody recognises her. I lean back, arms folded, showing distance.

"I want you to know that I'm happy, Alfie," she says through blue-painted lips. "I've got everything I ever wanted." But her voice sounds cold. It sounds haunted, like she is talking from the bottom of a deep dark pit.

"Really? Are you sure?"

"Why do you think I wouldn't be?"

"Because you don't have any control over your life any more. You're driven from one place to another in Magnus Gold's cars. You have to wear what he says, say what he tells you in interviews. You have to bribe drivers to be allowed out on your own. You don't even know what you are."

She frowns, sips her smoothie through a red straw. "That's not true."

"Of course it is. *What is Maya?* Who really knows what Maya is, what she does?"

"Keep your voice *down*," she hisses, looking round the bustling café. But nobody is paying us any attention. People with electric-blue wigs and shades probably come in here all the time. And my voice was partly drowned by the hiss of the coffee machine anyway.

I tick things off on my fingers. "You've recorded an album which is probably mostly a lot of session singers, and where it's you, you've been over-produced and auto-tuned so hard you can barely hear your own voice. You've released a fashion book which was ghosted. You've got your name on shoes you've supposedly designed, pencil-cases, make-up, T-shirts…"

She holds her hands up. "That's just the way it is now."

"Is it?" If that's true, I feel sad. My phone buzzes and I glance at it idly.

"Don't let me keep you from anything, Alfie," she says coldly.

It's a message from Liam.

want some inside info on your friend?

I feel myself turning hot and cold. It feels illicit, wrong. Maya is sitting in front of me and Liam is talking about her behind her back.

My finger hovers over the keyboard.

"You know what, Alfie?" she says. "I think you're just jealous. You're jealous of my ticket out of Greenwell Heights. You're jealous because I got to make something of my life, while you still have to live with your mum and do a boring BTEC at the crap local college. You know what? This was a mistake. I don't need friends like you, Alfie. I should never have come back here."

The words wash over me. Or at least that's what I pretend. Not looking up, I text back.

go on then

And when I look up, Maya has gone. Her chair is still wobbling, and her smoothie sits there, half-finished.

I gasp, slam some money down on the table and run out into the street.

The honey-gold cathedral looms in front of me. Business-people with sandwiches bustle back and forth, mums with pushchairs. I look up and down the street. There's no sign of her.

I glance at my phone again.

***

Half an hour later, I slam my bag down on a table in the college social area. Liam is sprawled there, hair flopping over his eyes, looking smug.

"This had better be good," I tell him. "'Too hot to text?' What does that even mean?"

Liam leans forward, cupping his hands. "OK. Listen up, Alfie. You know you're a really cool guy. You know I care about you."

I scowl. I can't look at him. "Flattery gets you everywhere."

"I don't like seeing you unhappy," he says. "I know you care about Maya. And, look, this may all be gossip, but…"

"What?" I perk up, leaning forward.

"That Magnus Gold, right. He's not exactly what you'd call ethical."

I snort. "Tell me something new. He's the man who got a cat meowing Christmas carols to Number One last Christmas, isn't he? He probably thinks *Ethics* is a place north of London."

Despite himself, Liam gives a little crooked smile. "There are these… rumours on the net about him. Do you know CrashAndBurn.com?"

"God, yeah."

C&B is the ultimate gossip site. It's a mixture of a forum. A blog and links to cheeky rumours and stuff which should really be getting them into trouble. It has come close to being shut down on a few occasions. It goes where even Perez Hilton and Blind Gossip fear to tread. It's run by this guy and his sister somewhere in Denmark.

"This is what happened, according to Harri," Liam says. Harri — that's the C&B girl, Harriet Mortensen. "They're saying Gold had a bet with one of his mates in the industry."

"A bet?" I feel my blood run cold.

"Yeah. They think it was Loz Campton, or Ken Starnes. One of those record industry guys. It doesn't really matter who. Gold bet them a million dollars that he could take someone, anyone — a complete unknown — and make them a multi-media star across several platforms in just a few months."

"But why her? Why Maya?" I ask.

"Perfect material," says Liam. He's obviously guessed that I'd think of asking this. He's been thinking it through, working it out. "I mean, they wanted someone ordinary, someone from... well, not a rich background. But someone pretty, with a natural charm. I reckon Gold and Silver went through hundreds of YouTubers and bloggers before they found the right person."

"The right person…" I repeat.

"Gold bet he could have the whole of the UK and Europe knowing their name. Buying their products without even really knowing what they do."

I feel myself turning cold and pale. I shut my eyes.

For a second, I remember the first day I met Maya, in Reception at school. Both of us in the colourful corner stacking plastic blocks, laughing. She wore a pink headband. My hair was still brown, and too long and scruffy. I remember wearing a shirt that was too big and smelled of detergent. And Jess Byars was sick all over Miss Kendrick's computer and we all laughed, falling over laughing while going, "Uuuuuugh!"

"Alfie?" Liam is waving a hand in front of my face. "Still with me?"

"Yes, sorry." I lean forward urgently. "Is she… reliable? This Harri girl?"

Liam grins. "Well, she was right about Esther Kay and Devon Chrome being a showmance. And Chezz Vance being married to Hector Watts just for the status, and to cover up that he's gay."

"Blimey. She exposed both of those?"

"Yup."

"What a bitch."

Liam and I laugh together. It's a good sound. "In this case," he says, "a bitch who is very useful to us. Shall I tell you what else she knows?"

I sip my Coke cautiously. "Go on."

"The other part of Gold's bet was that he could not only build someone up as a star, but destroy them within a month."

The world seems to tilt on its axis. I gaze into Liam's dark, earnest eyes. I think about that website, so many hundreds of miles away. I imagine streams of pixels like Tube trains through a dark tunnel, picture myself riding on them through Liam's eyes, through cyber-space until we reach Denmark, where Harri Mortensen sits at her laptop. (I picture her with very blonde hair, cropped short like Amber Rose. Dunno why.) And she grins and waves, and blows me a kiss across the North Sea. From Copenhagen with love.

"There's nothing we can do," I say. "Is there?"

Liam stirs his lime juice with his straw, flutters his eyelashes and grins. "Perhaps," he says. "Perhaps not."

***

That Friday, Maya's album plummets in the Official Charts from Number 2 to Number 46. Her awful auto-tuned single, 'Promises', disappears without trace from the radio playlists and isn't even available to view on YouTube or listen to on Spotify any more.

Comments appear online about her. Typical below-the-line stuff. Too horrible to repeat. Stuff about her appearance, her sexuality, her talent — or lack of it. Trolls-R-Us are up and running. Nasty pieces of work for hire.

There is a story — a terrible, nasty story — about her being involved in a homophobic incident at a club. It won't be, can't be true. But someone only has to print it, and have it believed…

Magnus Gold has moved into the final phase.

Project Annihilate Maya is in full swing.

He even appears on News 24. Showbiz reporters have hunted him down at some club, and he's there with his shades and his gleaming teeth, pushing through the throng. His face blank. "I have no comment to make on the career of Maya Barnes at this time."

He's never used her surname before. She was always one name, like Madonna, Zoella, Adele.

That's when I know it's over.

CHAPTER 6

BACKLASH

There's one final thing left to do.

I go online that night and I'm not surprised to find I no longer have a Twitter or Instagram account. Well, given the pretty uncomplimentary things I said about Magnus Gold — I couldn't resist, sorry, Liam — I'm not surprised.

I don't really care, to be honest.

Later that night, I Skype with Harri Mortensen of CrashAndBurn. Liam set it up for me. She doesn't look anything like I imagined. About as far from Amber Rose as she could be. She's small, snub-nosed, with raven-black hair and cool blue glasses. Not much older than me, I'm guessing.

"People like Gold," she says, with barely a trace of an accent, "you gotta realise they're untouchable, Alfie. But there's stuff we can do. *Bits and bobs*, yeah? Is that the right phrase?"

"Yes," I say with a grin. "Really? You can put stuff out there that'll harm someone as powerful as Magnus Gold?"

She sighs. "I dunno. In showbiz terms, the guy is Fort Knox, yeah? But he's got one thing going against him. He's forty-two, yeah? Forty-three, something like that? He doesn't quite get the modern world. Tumblr? That's a thing he drinks his scotch out of."

I laugh. "But what about his team?"

"Oh, yeah, he'll be surrounded by advisers. But I'm onto it. There's something we can do. There are things that hurt the rich and powerful. And it's not about money."

"Right."

I don't know what it is about.

"Reputation, Alfie," she says, spelling it out. "What people think of them, basically. That's everything to people like Gold. They wanna be liked. They wanna be adored."

"OK."

"Don't under-estimate the power of networks, Alfie. The people I know, they're strong together. They can do stuff."

I don't find out until the following week. When something else happens.

"Alfie!" My sister calls from the other room. "Someone for you."

I put my revision notes down and shamble through, rubbing my eyes. "Who is it?"

Kate, with her feet up watching *Take Me Out*, doesn't even turn to look at me. She just gestures with one red-painted fingernail. Pointing towards the hallway.

"What?" I ask, confused. There's nobody else in the flat.

"Downstairs," she says. "She didn't want to come up."

***

The putrid stairwell spirals away beneath me. Right at the bottom, looking up as if into a vortex, I see a small pale face framed by dark hair.

It takes me just under a minute to walk down to her.

"Why didn't you come in?" I ask, sitting on the steps.

Maya shrugs. She still looks cool, sleek — hair glossy, make-up immaculate, wearing a red leather biker jacket and a smart skirt and heels. Her hair is shorter and lighter, and she's got her normal glasses on again. No need for a disguise.

"Not sure I was welcome," she says.

"So how are things?" I ask.

She shrugs. "Pretty rough. Magnus's management dumped me. All kinds of nasty stuff took off, then.'

"What kind of thing?" I ask, curious. I have a vague idea. I've read a lot of it. But there's some I couldn't bring myself to read.

"Stuff in the paper and blogs that Gold's people didn't deny. Things went downhill pretty quickly after that."

I try to imagine what life is like, back in the real world, for someone whose entire existence has been managed for her. Money will not have existed for Maya. Washing-machines and supermarkets will not have existed. Chatting with her mates online will not have existed. Thanks to Magnus Gold's fleet of cars and drivers, even *rain* will not have existed.

"You seen this?" she says, holding up her phone.

It's on the BBC News site. There's a photo of Magnus Gold in full medallion-man mode, all bling and chest hair, with reporters all around him. I peer at the headline.

"'GOLD'S DRINK AND DRUGS SHAME'. You're kidding?"

I skim the story — something about a hotel in Amsterdam, and Gold being caught up in a police raid. It all sounds very sensational and OTT.

But, you know. People believe this stuff.

"He's not like that," she says. "I mean, yeah, he's selfish, and mean and arrogant, but… he'd never get mixed up in that. He protected me from all that."

She has no idea. She hasn't been online, hasn't seen the stuff on CrashAndBurn. She hasn't seen the stuff all the other sites. The stuff all Harri Mortensen's mates have been retweeting. Exposing Magnus Gold's little game, his little bet. It's caused quite a tidal wave of outrage over the past few days.

This, then, is social media's revenge, I guess. A second caught in time. Magnus Gold in a tabloid drink-and-drugs sting. And there's nothing in it — I trust what Maya's told me — but in this day and age, that kind of stuff… It sticks.

I imagine him up there somewhere in his helicopter, soaring above the city and the lights and all the normal people.

Rising above it all maybe.

"So," I say to Maya, "what you gonna do?"

She looks sheepish, pulling the jacket around her slender form. "Any places going on the BTEC?" she says, and laughs.

***

We're in the park again.

Weirdly, there's a girl of about ten on the climbing frame wearing a Maya T-shirt. She doesn't even notice who's on the swings, kicking high, laughing with the boy with green hair.

"Remember this?" I ask her, scraping the swing to a halt, offering my phone. We share the earphones.

Her songs. Her real songs. In her fragile voice, her real voice. 'Kill Me With Your Kiss', and 'Rivers of Memory' and all the rest.

She blushes. "Alfie, you kept them!"

"Of course I did. Gold couldn't take that away from you."

"Oh, Alfie," she says, and kisses me on the lips.

It's quite nice. But, no.

She draws back, her palms flat on my cheeks. "Still nothing?" she says, only half-joking.

"No!"

"I can actually do something with these, you know. Remember Zoe Silver?" Maya asks.

"The main man's enforcer? How could I forget?"

"Yeah, well, don't tell anyone this, but — she's told me she's going to set up on her own. Under her real name. Zoe Johnson Enterprises. She's had enough of the way Magnus Gold does things. She wants to curate small indie labels, experimental work, that kind of thing."

"Oh, *curate*. Bit poncy."

"Yeah well, she is a bit poncy. There's room for that in the world, though, Alfie. People aren't black and white."

We laugh, and kick off on the swings again, and we're riding high, kicking up to the sky. The blocks of Greenwell Heights in the distance and the song playing in our heads.

You never forget it when you first feel like this...

THE END

ABOUT THE AUTHOR

Daniel Blythe is the author of 20 books, including several of the *Doctor Who* novels, as well as *Shadow Runners* and *Emerald Greene and the Witch Stones*. He is originally from Maidstone, but now lives with his wife and teenage children in Yorkshire. He has been published in 12 countries including the USA, Germany and Brazil, and he has led writing days and workshops in over 400 schools.